Asterix and the Great Divide

British Library Cataloguing in Publication Data

A catalogue record for this book is available from the British Library

ISBN 0-340-25988-4 (cased)
ISBN 0-340-27627-4 (limp)

Original edition © Les Editions Albert René, Goscinny-Uderzo, 1980
English translation: © Les Editions Albert René, Goscinny-Uderzo, 1981
Exclusive Licensee: Hodder and Stoughton Ltd
Translators: Anthea Bell and Derek Hockridge

First published in Great Britain 1981 (cased)
This impression 120 119 118 117 116 115 114
First published in Great Britain 1982 (limp)
This impression 120

Published by Hodder Children's Books,
a division of Hodder Headline
338 Euston Road, London NW1 3BH.

Printed in Belgium by Proost International Book Production

GOSCINNY AND UDERZO
PRESENT
AN ASTERIX ADVENTURE

ASTERIX
AND THE
GREAT DIVIDE

WRITTEN AND ILLUSTRATED BY UDERZO
TRANSLATED BY ANTHEA BELL AND DEREK HOCKRIDGE

Hodder
Children's
Books

a division of Hodder Headline

GOSCINNYRIX · VDERZORIX

VIS COMICA*

* The power to make people laugh: from an epigram by Caesar on Terence, the Latin poet.

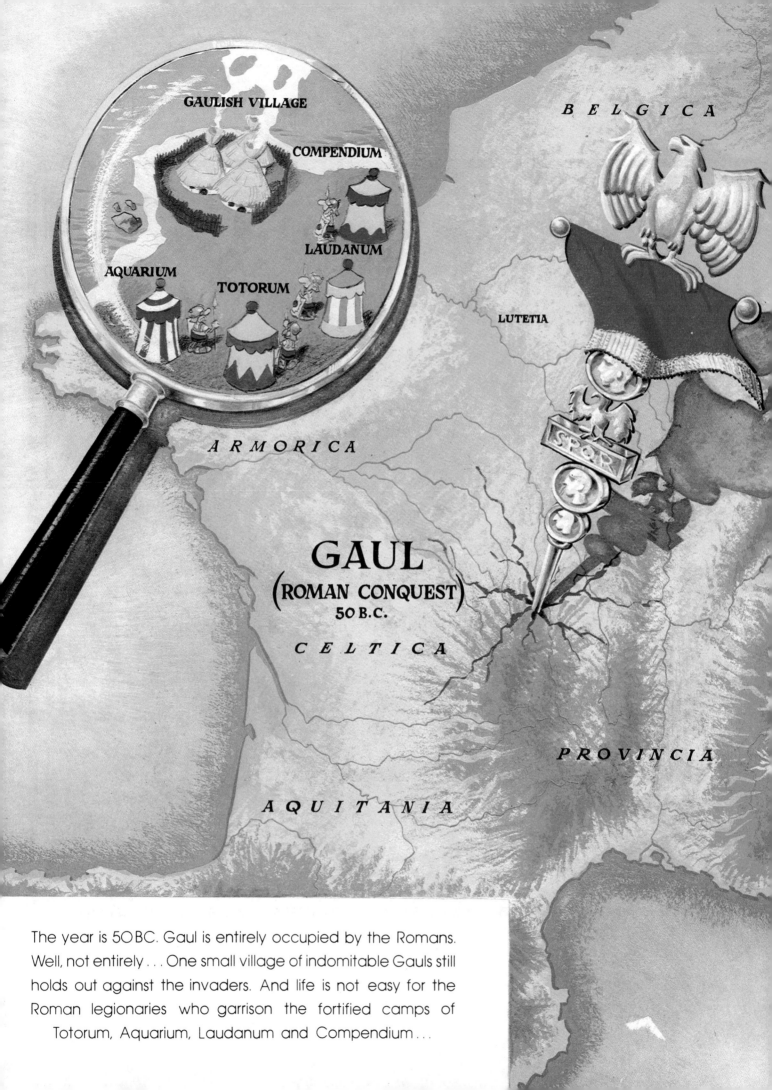

GAUL
(ROMAN CONQUEST)
50 B.C.

The year is 50 BC. Gaul is entirely occupied by the Romans. Well, not entirely... One small village of indomitable Gauls still holds out against the invaders. And life is not easy for the Roman legionaries who garrison the fortified camps of Totorum, Aquarium, Laudanum and Compendium...

SOMEWHERE IN GAUL, PEACE WOULD BE REIGNING IN A LITTLE VILLAGE VERY LIKE THE VILLAGE WHERE ASTERIX LIVES...

...BUT FOR VARIOUS PECULIAR INCIDENTS. A BIG DITCH HAS BEEN DUG THROUGH THE MIDDLE OF THE VILLAGE, SO THAT NO ONE CAN GET FROM THE RIGHT SIDE TO THE LEFT SIDE.

CLEVERDIX HAS BEEN ELECTED CHIEF BY THE LEFT OF THE VILLAGE...

NEVER MIND WHAT THE OTHER LOT SAY, I'VE BEEN UNANIMOUSLY ELECTED VILLAGE CHIEF!

MAJESTIX HAS BEEN ELECTED CHIEF BY THE RIGHT OF THE VILLAGE...MONARCH OF HALF HE SURVEYS.

BY DIVINE RIGHT!

5

VARIOUS ATTEMPTS HAVE BEEN MADE TO DEAL WITH THE SITUATION...

AND THE VILLAGERS OF THE LEFT AND THE RIGHT ARE EVER READY TO EXPRESS THEIR MUTUAL ANTAGONISM.

RSPRR! RSPRR!

BUT IT WOULD TAKE POSITIVELY SINISTER DEXTERITY TO SOLVE CERTAIN VITAL PROBLEMS...

?!

?!

...AND ONLY THE CHILDREN ARE ANY BETTER OFF FOR THE RIFT.

SCRUNCH!

YOU'VE GOT NO RIGHT TO DO THAT! THAT'S MY TREE!!!

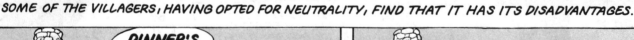

SOME OF THE VILLAGERS, HAVING OPTED FOR NEUTRALITY, FIND THAT IT HAS ITS DISADVANTAGES.

DINNER'S READY!

COMING, DARLING!

BONK!

IN CHIEF CLEVERDIX'S HUT...

LOOK HERE, FATHER, THIS CAN'T GO ON! THAT DITCH DIVIDING US IS A DISGRACE TO THE VILLAGE!

IS THAT MY FAULT, HISTRIONIX, MY BOY? THAT TRAITOR MAJESTIX SANK TO BRIBING SOME OF THE VOTERS!

HE AND HIS HENCHMAN, THE UNSPEAKABLE CODFIX, HAD THE NERVE TO GET VOTES FROM VILLAGERS WHO WERE ONLY BABES IN ARMS!

WELL, AT THIS RATE FUTURE GENERATIONS OF GAULS AREN'T GOING TO THINK MUCH OF THEIR ANCESTORS!

CAN YOU SUGGEST ANYTHING, FATHER?

YES, MY BOY, I CAN. I'VE DECIDED TO MAKE A SPEECH TO THE VILLAGERS OPPOSITE. THAT'LL BRIDGE THE GAP. THEY'LL SOON SEE HOW WRONG THEY WERE TO DITCH ME!

AND IN CHIEF MAJESTIX'S HUT...

OH, FATHER, DO YOU REMEMBER HOW HAPPY THE VILLAGE WAS WHEN WE ONLY HAD ONE CHIEF, ALTRUISTIX?

YES, I DO! THE OLD SO-AND-SO TOOK AFTER HIS COUSIN ALCAPONIX... MAKING OFF WITH ALL THE VILLAGE'S TAXES!

THIS IS ALL THAT FOOL CLEVERDIX'S FAULT! HE STOLE VOTES WHICH WERE MINE BY RIGHT.

HE EVEN PROMISED TO BRING DOWN INFLATION, AND THOSE IDIOTS FELL FOR IT! THAT WAS WHEN THE BALLOON WENT UP!

MELODRAMA IS RIGHT! WE NEED A SINGLE CHIEF TO LEAD THE VILLAGE. YOU LET THEM KNOW OVER ON THE LEFT THAT YOU'RE THE RIGHTFUL CHIEF!

CODFIX, YOUR ADVICE ISN'T ALWAYS CODSWALLOP! YES, I'LL ADDRESS THEM!

AND SOON AFTERWARDS...

9

ELSEWHERE, PEACE IS REIGNING IN ANOTHER LITTLE VILLAGE, A VILLAGE WE ALL KNOW WELL...

LOOK, IF PEACE IS REIGNING IN OUR LITTLE VILLAGE, THE VILLAGE THEY ALL KNOW WELL, THAT MEANS THE ROMANS ARE SULKING, ASTERIX!

NO, OBELIX, IT JUST MEANS THEY'VE LEARNT A BIT OF SENSE!

?!

WHAT ARE YOU DOING ON THAT CONTRAPTION, O CHIEF VITAL-STATISTIX?

ER...WELL...I'M GOING OUT SHOPPING FOR IMPEDIMENTA. SHE'S FEELING A BIT UNDER THE WEATHER.

BUT WHAT'S THE CART FOR?

OH, THE CART! THAT'S A NEW IDEA OF MINE. IT MEANS THESE CLUMSY GREAT OAFS CAN'T LET ME DOWN ANY MORE WHEN THE FANCY TAKES THEM.

RIGHT, YOU TWO! WHATEVER YOU DO NOW, I STAND FIRM ON MY TRUSTY SHIELD! SO OFF WE GO SHOPPING!

BONG!

SIGH

AND HE CAN'T SHOP US FOR THAT, OR GET NEW SHIELD-BEARERS...

NO, WE SHIELD-BEARERS OPERATE A CLOSED SHOP!

DOWNCAST AGAIN, PIGGYWIGGY? THINKING YOURSELF SO CLEVER... HUH! PIGS MIGHT FLY!

BY BELENOS, SO YOU'RE STILL THE FALL GUY, CHIEF VITALSTATISTIX?

SHUT UP AND SERVE ME! AND FAST! YOU COULD CUT THE ATMOSPHERE AROUND HERE WITH A KNIFE!

AND JUST WHAT DO YOU MEAN BY THAT?

I MEAN YOU GET A THUMP UP THE HOOTER IF YOU DON'T HURRY UP, THAT'S WHAT!!

NOW, LADDIE, THE THING IS TO STRIKE WHILE THE IRON IS...

BIFF!

BANG BANG!

...HOT...

SPLATCH!

AND HERE'S A STRIKING EXAMPLE OF ACTING IN THE HEAT OF THE MOMENT!

BIFF! BANG!

PLATCH!

GERIATRIX, SWEETIE-PIE, DON'T GO FAR! DINNER'S NEARLY READY!

JUST TAKING SOME EXERCISE TO WORK UP AN APPETITE!

THESE GAULS ARE CRAZY!

BIFF! BING! BANG!

TOK! TOK! TOK!

SPLOTCH!

I CAN'T KEEP A FISH WHICH DOESN'T BELONG TO ME, CAN I, ASTERIX? I'LL RETURN IT TO THE OWNER WHILE YOU GET DINNER!

DINNER'S READY!

DINNER'S READY!

DINNER'S READY!

DINNER'S READY!

DINNER'S READY!

DINNER'S READY!

DINNER'S READY!

DINNER'S READY!

LISTEN, WHY DON'T WE CARRY ON LATER TO HELP OUR DINNER DOWN?

AND MEANWHILE, WOULD YOU MIND HELPING *ME* DOWN? MY WIFE'S WAITING!

THESE FISH ARE ALMOST PAST IT, EVEN FOR HELPING PEOPLE RELAX. CHANGE AND DECAY IN ALL AROUND I SEE...

NIGHT HAS FALLEN, AND ALL IS CALM AGAIN IN THE VILLAGE.

TIME FOR BED, SCHIZO-PHRENIX!

COMING, DARLING!

BONG!

CODFIX IS GOING TO ASK THE ROMANS TO HELP MAKE MY FATHER CHIEF OF THE WHOLE VILLAGE...AND IN RETURN MY FATHER HAS PROMISED HIM MY HAND IN MARRIAGE!

HOW DARE HE?! BUT I'M FROM THE OPPOSITE CAMP, MELODRAMA...WHY ARE YOU TELLING ME ALL THIS?

BECAUSE YOU'RE THE ONLY PERSON WITH ANY SENSE IN THIS CRAZY VILLAGE, AND I DON'T WANT TO MARRY CODFIX! O HISTRIONIX, HISTRIONIX! WHEREFORE ART THOU HISTRIONIX?

!?!

RAISE THE ALARM!

BONK!

ARE YOU HURT, HISTRIONIX?

NO, I'M ALL RIGHT... I FANCY A PASSING SHOAL OF FISH BROKE MY FALL!

*GIRLS CURRIED FAVOUR WITH THIS GODDESS

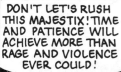

11ª

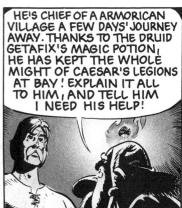

11B

15

...AND THAT, O CHIEF VITALSTATISTIX, IS THE SAD STORY OF OUR VILLAGE. ONLY YOUR DRUID GETAFIX'S MAGIC POTION AND THE WISDOM OF YOUR EXPERIENCED WARRIORS CAN SAVE US!

HMPH, YES. SPEAKING OF THE WISDOM OF MY EX-PERIENCED WARRIORS, I SOME-HOW FEEL I SHOULD BE PUTTING MY OWN HOUSE IN ORDER FIRST...

...BUT SINCE THE ROMANS LOOK LIKE GETTING MIXED UP IN YOUR AFFAIRS, I DON'T SEE WHY I SHOULDN'T LEND MY OLD COMRADE-IN-ARMS CLEVERDIX A HAND!

THANK YOU... AND ON MY OWN BEHALF TOO! UNLESS WE FIND A PEACEFUL SOLUTION, MELODRAMA AND I CAN NEVER HOPE TO BE UNITED!

BOO HOO HOO

?

BOO HOO HOO HOO

WHAT'S THE MATTER, OBELIX?

SNIFF! I GET ALL UPSET BY LOVE STORIES WITH UNHAPPY ENDINGS! SNIFF!

HUH!

BUT THIS STORY'S ONLY JUST BEGINNING, AND IF CHIEF VITALSTATISTIX WILL LET US, WE'RE GOING TO HELP HISTRIONIX SOLVE HIS PROBLEMS!

OOH, YES, LET'S! GOODY, GOODY, GOODY!

WOOF! WOOF!

THE ROMANS AROUND HERE ARE KEEPING VERY QUIET JUST NOW, SO I THINK I CAN JOIN THE EXPEDITION MYSELF! THE PEOPLE OF YOUR VILLAGE MAY NEED ME TO HELP THEM BRIDGE THE GREAT DIVIDE!

AND A LITTLE LATER...

WILL HE SING? WON'T HE SING? WILL HE SING? WON'T HE SING?

IN THE ROMAN CAMP NEAR THE DIVIDED VILLAGE...

HEY, SOURPUS, I'LL SWAP YOU TWO SENTRY DUTIES FOR ONE LAUNDRY FATIGUE!

NOTHING DOING! YOU ALREADY OWE ME THREE COOKHOUSE FATIGUES AND TWO LATRINE FATIGUES!

BACK AT THE RECRUITMENT OFFICE, THEY TOLD US WE'D GET BEAUTIFUL SLAVE-GIRLS FROM THE COUNTRIES WE CONQUERED...

BACK IN ROME, CAESAR SAID HE WAS COUNTING ON US TO CLEAN UP THE BARBARIANS...WHAT A WASH-OUT!

LOOT, THEY SAID. THE CARROT FOR THE DONKEY!

IT'S A MAN'S LIFE IN THE ARMY, THEY SAID...

ALL RIGHT, WE KNOW, WE KNOW!

DECURION INFECTIUS VIRUS, THIS TENT IS A PIGSTY, AND THE COOKING IN THE CAMP IS GOING FROM BAD TO WORSE!

I KNOW. THE COOKHOUSE IS REVOLTING, O CENTURION UMBRAGEOUS CUMULONIMBUS. THERE'S A MOOD OF GENERAL UNREST. THE MEN WANT SLAVES TO DO THE DIRTY WORK, BUT CAESAR SAID WE WEREN'T TO TAKE SLAVES DURING THE ROMAN PEACE!

WISH I'D BROUGHT MY SLAVEGIRL FROM HOME...NICE LITTLE ROMAN PIECE*, SHE IS!

* PAX ROMANA

CENTURION, I HAVE THE ANSWER TO ALL YOUR PROBLEMS!

?!

WHO LET YOU INTO THIS CAMP, GAUL?

THE MAN ON DUTY AT THE GATE. HE WAS QUITE HAPPY WHEN I OFFERED HIM A SLAVE IN EXCHANGE!

WHO ARE YOU, ANYWAY? HOW DARE YOU CORRUPT MY LEGIONARIES?

I'M FROM MAJESTIX, RIGHTFUL CHIEF OF THE RIGHT SIDE OF OUR VILLAGE. I'M HIS ALTER EGO AND RIGHT HAND!

TOK TOK

AND THIS IS MY LEFT FOOT! BE OFF, OR IT'LL ALTER *YOUR* EGO!

CHIEF MAJESTIX WANTS YOU TO HELP HIM PUT DOWN A REBELLION LED BY CLEVERDIX!

THAT'S NONE OF MY BUSINESS! THIS IS YOUR NUNC DIMITTIS...GET OUT, OR YOU'LL BE SINGING A DIFFERENT TUNE. A FUNERAL DIRGE FROM HYMNS ANCIENT*!

*HYMNS MODERN AS YET UNWRITTEN

HOLD ON A MOMENT, CENTURION! YOU HELP MY CHIEF, CLEVERDIX AND HIS MEN WILL BE CONQUERED ...SO YOU CAN MAKE THEM YOUR *SLAVES!* YOUR LEGIONARIES ARE VERY KEEN ON HAVING SLAVES!

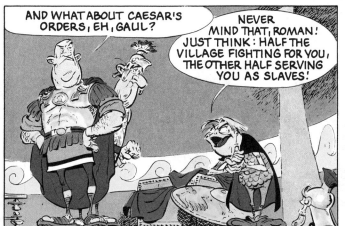

AND WHAT ABOUT CAESAR'S ORDERS, EH, GAUL?

NEVER MIND THAT, ROMAN! JUST THINK: HALF THE VILLAGE FIGHTING FOR YOU, THE OTHER HALF SERVING YOU AS SLAVES!

THAT'S ALL A LOAD OF COD! I'VE GOT OTHER FISH TO FRY. GET MOVING BEFORE I PUT YOU ON FATIGUES YOURSELF!

RESTORE OUR DIFFERENTIALS! GIVE US SLAVES!

LEGIONARIES' LIB!

NO MORE CHORES!

SCRUB THOSE SCRUBBING BRUSHES!

?!

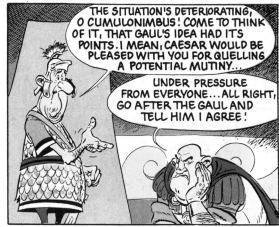

THE SITUATION'S DETERIORATING, O CUMULONIMBUS! COME TO THINK OF IT, THAT GAUL'S IDEA HAD ITS POINTS. I MEAN, CAESAR WOULD BE PLEASED WITH YOU FOR QUELLING A POTENTIAL MUTINY...

UNDER PRESSURE FROM EVERYONE... ALL RIGHT, GO AFTER THE GAUL AND TELL HIM I AGREE!

HALT! IF YOU WANT TO LEAVE THE CAMP YOU'LL HAVE TO PROMISE ME ANOTHER SLAVE!

WAIT A MOMENT, GAUL!

GO AND TELL YOUR CHIEF THAT WE'LL GIVE HIM THE HELP HE WANTS. JUST LET US HAVE TIME TO EXPLAIN IT ALL TO OUR LEGIONARIES!

HO, HO! MY VILLAINY KNOWS NO BOUNDS! AND I'M NOT THROUGH YET, BECAUSE WHEN I'VE MARRIED THE BEAUTIFUL MELODRAMA, IT WILL BE EASY ENOUGH FOR ME TO DEPOSE THAT FOOL MAJESTIX AND BECOME CHIEF OF THE VILLAGE MYSELF!

FUNNY, I COULD HAVE SWORN I SMELT SOMETHING FISHY!

SNIFF! SNIFF!

YOU KNOW, FATHER, MAJESTIX REALLY DID ACT IN A MANNER WORTHY OF A CHIEF!

ALL THINGS CONSIDERED, I MUST ADMIT HE CARRIED IT OFF IN STYLE!

WE'LL GET THEM THIS TIME, ASTERIX!!!

NO, OBELIX! IT COULD PUT MAJESTIX AND HIS WARRIORS IN DANGER!

A LITTLE LATER...

WE MUST DO SOMETHING, HISTRIONIX!

DON'T WORRY, MELODRAMA! IF MY FATHER WILL AGREE, WE'LL ORGANIZE A CAMPAIGN AGAINST THE ROMANS TO FREE OUR FELLOW VILLAGERS!

I CERTAINLY AGREE! MAJESTIX MAY BE MY OPPONENT, BUT I DON'T WANT HIM USING HIS SACRIFICE AS AN ARGUMENT AT THE POLLS!

HUH!

WAIT A MOMENT! I'VE GOT A BETTER IDEA!

THE ROMANS OF THESE PARTS DON'T KNOW GETAFIX, OBELIX AND ME. WE'LL GO TO THE ROMAN CAMP ON OUR OWN. IF IT'S SLAVES THEY WANT, WE'LL APPLY FOR THE JOB, AND SET THE PRISONERS FREE!

AN EXCELLENT IDEA, ASTERIX!

OOH, YES! GOODY, GOODY, GOODY! A CHANCE TO SAMPLE THE LOCAL ROMANS AT LAST...

CLAP! CLAP! CLAP!

...THUMPING ROMANS IS LIKE HAVING DINNER: IT'S NICE TO EAT OUT FOR A CHANGE!

IN THE ROMAN CAMP...

WE WILL NEVER BE YOUR SLAVES, ROMAN!

DO YOU KNOW THE PENALTIES FOR A SLAVES' REVOLT? YOU'D BETTER STOP AND THINK, UNLESS YOU WANT TO MAKE THE LIONS IN THE CIRCUS MAXIMUS AT ROME A SQUARE MEAL!

AND WHILE THEY'RE THINKING, CHAIN THEM ALL UP WELL!!!

CAN I HAVE THOSE THREE SENTRY DUTIES BACK? THE ONES YOU SWAPPED FOR MY COOKHOUSE FATIGUE!

PRICES HAVE RISEN... IT'LL BE FOUR SENTRY DUTIES NOW!

MEANWHILE...

GOOD LUCK, FRIENDS!

DON'T WORRY, MELODRAMA! THANKS TO GETAFIX'S KNOW-HOW, OBELIX'S STRENGTH, DOGMATIX'S NOSE AND MY CUNNING, WE'LL SOON HAVE YOUR FATHER HOME!

FUNNY HOW SURE OF THEMSELVES CLEVERDIX'S ALLIES SEEM! I'LL FOLLOW THE AT A SAFE DISTANCE!

DOGMATIX HAS BEEN SNIFFING ABOUT EVER SINCE WE LEFT! I THINK HE'S PICKED UP THE SCENT OF A BOAR!

NO, NO, IT'S JUST A RED HERRING.

SNIFF! SNIFF! SNIFF!

IF SO, IT'S BEEN TAKING CODLIVER OIL!

SNIFF! SNIFF!

RIGHT, YOU GET THE IDEA, OBELIX? WE'RE HUMBLE SLAVES, SO NO THUMPING THE ROMANS!

LISTEN, ASTERIX...

...IS THERE SUCH A THING AS A SLAVE-DOG?

23

24

GLUG GLUG GLUG

GLUG GLUG GLUG

NO, OBELIX, NOT YOU!

AND WHY NOT HIM?

YES, WHY NOT ME?

BECAUSE HE FELL INTO THE CAULDRON WHEN HE WAS A BABY, AND... ER... UM...

AND HE HAS TO STAY ON A STRICT DIET FOR THE GOOD OF HIS MENTAL HEALTH, THAT'S WHY NOT HIM!

DON'T WORRY, WE'RE HERE TO RESCUE YOU. THE POTION WILL GIVE YOU THE STRENGTH YOU NEED. WATCH FOR OUR SIGNAL! THEN YOU HAVE NOTHING TO LOSE BUT YOUR CHAINS!

?!

SOON AFTERWARDS...

YOU SEE, ROMAN, THE WAS NO NEED FOR YOU TO WORRY!

WELL, SINCE THERE ISN'T ANY SOUP LEFT, LET'S GO STRAIGHT ON TO THE NEXT COURSE ON THE MENU, WHICH IS...

THE CHOP!

THE MENU! I SEE IT ALL NOW!!!

SO DO WE! COME ON, MEN!

SNAP!

27

THAT POTION OF YOURS HAS A REALLY UPLIFTING EFFECT!

YES, IT USUALLY MAKES PEOPLE RISE TO THE OCCASION!

TRY A BIT OF KNUCKLE IN THE BREAD-BASKET FOR A CHANGE!

ENJOYING YOUR PICNIC AL FRESCO?

GRRRR

I GET THE PICTURE... NO NEED FOR ANY BIG FRESCO TO SHOW THAT THE ROMANS CAN'T STOMACH THAT DRUID'S RECIPES!

GAULISH COOKING! HUH! THEY CAN SCOFF THE LOT THEMSELVES!

PERSONALLY, I DON'T SEE ANYTHING TO SCOFF AT.

SSH! SHUT UP! THEY MIGHT WANT CARVE US UP SOME MORE.

I DON'T KNOW WHO YOU ARE, BUT THANKS VERY MUCH! YOU CAME IN THE NICK OF TIME!

I'M GETAFIX, AND MY FRIENDS HERE ARE ASTERIX, OBELIX AND DOGMATIX. CLEVERDIX SENT US!

CLEVERDIX WANTED TO FIGHT THE ROMANS WITH HIS OWN WARRIORS, BUT WE THOUGHT OUR METHODS WERE SUBTLER!

THERE'S SOMETHING TO BE SAID FOR THAT OLD ROGUE CLEVERDIX AFTER ALL!

NOW, LET'S GO BACK TO THE VILLAGE. AND I SHALL HAVE SOMETHING TO SAY TO THAT TRAITOR CODFIX!

OH, HELP! I'D BETTER LIE LOW FOR A WHILE!

HALT! SLAVES ARE NOT ALLOWED TO LEAVE THE CAMP!

THAT'S ALL RIGHT, WE'RE NOT SLAVES ANY MORE. WE'RE FREE GAULS AGAIN! YOU CAN LET US PASS!

HUH! AS LIARS GO, YOU'RE A FAT LOT OF GOOD!

LEAVE THIS TO ME, ASTERIX!

GOOD I MAY BE, BUT I... AM... NOT... FAT!

TCHAC!

JUST NICELY COVERED, THAT'S ALL.

WELL, YOU'RE CERTAINLY VERY THIN-SKINNED! COME ON, OBELIX!

O DRUID, WASN'T IT A BIT DANGEROUS TO GIVE THE ROMANS A CHANCE TO DRINK OUR MAGIC POTION TOO?

THAT WAS A RISK WE HAD TO TAKE. I HAD EVERY CONFIDENCE IN THE ROMANS' LACK OF CONFIDENCE IN US, ASTERIX!

OH, FATHER!

MELODRAMA, MY DEAR CHILD!

IT WAS ALL BECAUSE OF THAT DREADFUL CODFIX!

YES, AND WHERE'S THE TWO-TIMING SO-AND-SO NOW?

HE DISAPPEARED WHEN YOU LEFT.

HUH! HE'LL BE LOOKING PRETTY GREEN AROUND THE GILLS WHEN I FIND HIM!

YOU KNOW, I FEEL CODFIX MAY STILL BE FISHING IN THESE TROUBLED WATERS!

YES. WE DON'T WANT HIM TURNING THE SCALES...

OUR OWN QUARREL ISN'T SETTLED YET, YOU KNOW, YOU ROTTEN OLD FRAUD!

IT CERTAINLY ISN'T! AND THIS TIME IT'LL BE A FAIR FIGHT, YOU ROTTEN OLD OPPORTUNIST!

YES, WELL, MEANWHILE YOU'D BETTER BARRICADE YOUR-SELVES INSIDE THE VILLAGE, IN CASE THE ROMANS DECIDE TO COME BACK!

AND I'M GOING TO BREW UP SOME MAGIC POTION... ONLY TO BE TAKEN IF THE ROMANS DO COME BACK, OF COURSE!

26A

JUST AT THAT MOMENT, HOWEVER, THE ROMANS HAVE NOT RECOVERED FROM THEIR LITTLE SETBACK. MEANWHILE...

NOW THAT THE WHOLE VILLAGE IS AGAINST ME, I'D BETTER MAKE USE OF THE ROMANS TO SATISFY MY THIRST FOR VENGEANCE...

...AND A FEW DROPS OF THE DRUID'S ELIXIR, ADDED TO THIS WINE, WILL HELP ME WHEN THE CENTURION COMES TO SATISFY HIS THIRST!

SOUND THE ASSEMBLY!

26B

RIGHT! WE SHALL NOW FORGET THIS WHOLE UNFORTUNATE EPISODE AND CLEAR UP THE MESS! I WANT THE GARRISON ALL SPRUCED UP AND LOOKING LIKE A **CENA CANIS***! DISMISS!

*LATIN: DOG'S DINNER

WHAT'S CENA CANIS?

DOG LATIN, YOU IDIOT!

AH, A NICE GOBLET OF WINE WILL HELP ME FORGET MY TROUBLES!

GLUG! GLUG! GLUG!

AAAH! BY JUPITER, I'M FEELING ON TOP OF THE WORLD!

?!? WHO ARE YOU, GAUL, AND WHO LET YOU INTO THIS CAMP?

IT'S WORKING!

I'VE COME TO WARN YOU, O CENTURION! THE GAULS OF THE NEARBY VILLAGE HAVE BROKEN THE PAX ROMANA! THEY'VE BASHED UP YOUR LEGIONARIES AND RANSACKED YOUR CAMP!

IMPOSSIBLE! OR ARE YOU GIVING ME SOME INSIDE DOPE?

O CUMULONIMBUS, THE MEN DON'T WANT TO CLEAR UP THE MESS! THEY'RE ALL REPORTING SICK!

SICK BAY

AND LATER...

I STILL HAVE NO IDEA WHO YOU ARE, GAUL, BUT YOU WON'T FIND ME UNGRATEFUL FOR SERVICES RENDERED!

WE CAN TALK ABOUT THAT LATER, ONCE YOU'VE DONE FOR THE VILLAGE AND ALL ITS INHABITANTS.

BUT WATCH OUT! THERE'S A DRUID WITH THEM, AND HE HAS A POTION WHICH MAKES ANYONE WHO DRINKS IT INVINCIBLE!

CENTURION, A COUSIN OF MINE STATIONED IN ARMORICA TOLD ME ABOUT A DRUID THERE WHO HAS STRANGE POWERS, AND I'M JUST WONDERING WHETHER...

YOU'VE GOT A POINT, INFECTIUS VIRUS! WE MUST BE CAREFUL!

MEANWHILE, IN THE GAULISH VILLAGE...

THE MAGIC POTION'S READY. WE'D BETTER PUT IT SAFE ON NEUTRAL GROUND SOMEWHERE WHILE WE WAIT TO SEE IF THE ROMANS ARE COMING BACK!

SCHIZOPHRENIX'S HUT IS NEUTRAL GROUND. IT'S BANG IN THE MIDDLE OF THE VILLAGE.

YES, LET'S PUT IT THERE. THAT FOOL SCHIZOPHRENIX HAS NEVER BEEN ABLE TO DECIDE WHICH SIDE HE'S ON!

DIDN'T YOU EVER THINK OF PUTTING FLOOR- BOARDS DOWN OVER THE GAP?

THAT'S FLOORED HIM! WE'LL DO IT NOW.

AND SO, A LITTLE LATER...

I'LL WATCH OVER THE CAULDRON TONIGHT, TO MAKE DOUBLY SURE!

THEN YOU'D BETTER HAVE THIS GOURD OF MAGIC POTION, ASTERIX. YOU NEVER KNOW, YOU MIGHT NEED A BOOSTER DOSE, IN SPITE OF THE POTION IN THE CAULDRON.

AND THAT NIGHT, ON THE OUTSKIRTS OF THE WOOD NEAR THE GAULISH VILLAGE...

I DON'T TRUST THAT DRUID AND HIS SECRET WEAPONS! I THINK I'D BETTER GO SCOUTING AHEAD BEFORE WE ATTACK!

AND WHATEVER YOU DO, DON'T MOVE TILL I GET BACK!

RIGHT, BUT HURRY UP! I CAN'T WAIT TO GET MY REVENGE ON THOSE GAULS!

THE GODS OF THE UNDERWORLD ARE ON MY SIDE! IT'S THAT FOOL CONGENITAL-IDIOTIX ON SENTRY DUTY! I'LL SOON DEAL WITH HIM!

HALT! WHO GOES THERE?

IT'S ME. CODFIX.

I MIGHT HAVE KNOWN FROM THE SMELL! WHAT DO YOU WANT?

I WANT TO ASK CHIEF MAJESTIX TO FORGIVE ME!

YOU CAN COME IN, BUT IF I WERE YOU I'D KEEP MY DISTANCE FROM MAJESTIX!

WHY ARE YOU MOUNTING GUARD LIKE THIS? WHAT ARE YOU AFRAID OF?

WE'RE AFRAID THE ROMANS MAY COME BACK. BUT LUCKILY GETAFIX THE DRUID HAS MADE US SOME OF HIS MAGIC POTION. IT'S SAFE IN SCHIZO-PHRENIX'S HUT!

TEEHEE!

I'VE NEVER BEEN ABLE TO SEE STARS INSIDE A HUT BEFORE!

BONG!

I'M SURE I SHALL NEED SOME OF THIS!

I FEEL QUITE SORRY FOR COD-FIX, APOLOGIZING TO THE CHIEF... HE MUST BE HAVING TO STEEL HIMSELF. WONDER IF HE'LL GET AWAY WITH IT?

?!

CRAAASH!

HELP! HELP!

DO SOMETHING, GETAFIX! GIVE HIM SOME OF THE ELIXIR YOU USED ON THE ROMANS!

I'M SORRY, MY DEAR OBELIX, I'M AFRAID I MUST HAVE LEFT IT NEAR THE ROMAN CAMP!

ANYWAY, IT WOULD BE DANGEROUS TO GIVE IT TO ASTERIX. ANYONE WHO DRINKS MY ELIXIR CAN'T TAKE THE MAGIC POTION AFTER-WARDS... THE MIXTURE HAS SOME RATHER STRANGE EFFECTS!

BUT LUCKILY ASTERIX IS ALL RIGHT!

THIS TIME I REALLY DO THINK THE SKY HAS FALLEN ON MY HEAD!

THE SKY'S FALLEN ON EVERYONE'S HEAD, ASTERIX! CODFIX HAS STOLEN THE MAGIC POTION, AND HE'S SURE TO DOSE THE ROMANS WITH IT.

HUH! MAGIC POTION OR NO MAGIC POTION, WE CAN DEAL WITH THE ROMANS!

SPOKEN LIKE THE TRUE SON OF A CHIEF!

HMPH!

36

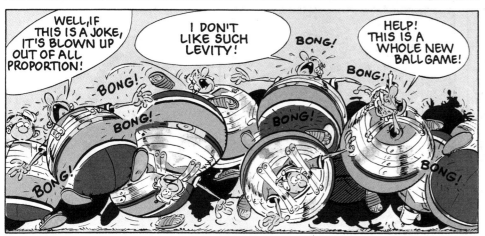

THESE ROMANS
ARE REALLY CRAZY!
THEY'RE NOT AT
THE CIRCUS
NOW!

AND
MEANWHILE...

BING!

BANG!

BONG!

AHA! NO MORE GLOBE-TROTTING! WE'RE BACK TO NORMAL!

PICK UP YOUR WEAPONS AND GET BACK TO BATTLE STATIONS!!!

O CUMULONIMBUS, I'M AN OLD SOLDIER, AND I'VE BEEN AROUND, BUT I'VE NEVER FOUGHT IN TERRAIN QUITE LIKE THIS!

I'LL TELL YOU ANOTHER FUNNY THING... WE'VE LOST SIGHT OF THE ENEMY!

BUT WE'RE STILL HERE, O ROMAN!

?!?

EEEEK!

WELL, MY DEAR OBELIX, YOU STARTED QUITE A TRAIN OF EVENTS WITH THAT PUNCH YOU GAVE THE SENTRY OUTSIDE THE ROMAN CAMP... AND THE ENEMY LOST OUT!

YOU MEAN I DID IT?

ER... MAJESTIX, NOW WE'VE DEALT WITH THE ROMANS, I... THERE'S SOMETHING I'D LIKE TO ASK YOU...

JUST A MOMENT, MY BOY! DON'T FORGET YOUR FATHER AND I STILL HAVE TO SETTLE OUR ARGUMENT, AND...

MAJESTIX! MAJESTIX!

?!

CODFIX HAS KIDNAPPED MELODRAMA! HE LEFT THIS ROLL OF PARCHMENT ADDRESSED TO YOU!

THE DOUBLE-DEALING TRAITOR!

37^A

IF YOU WANT TO SEE MELODRAMA AGAIN, LEAVE 100 POUNDS IN GOLD NEAR THE DOLMEN BY THE SPRING BEFORE SUNSET.

Codfix

THE VILLAIN! I'M REALLY IN A JAM NOW, AND SO IS MELODRAMA... IT'S ALL VERY WELL FOR CODFIX*, BUT WHERE DO I GET THAT KIND OF MONEY BY SUNSET?

I SHALL LEAVE AT ONCE IN SEARCH OF CODFIX, AND BY TOUTATIS, I SWEAR TO BRING MELODRAMA BACK SAFE AND SOUND!

* HENCE: MONEY FOR JAM.

OBELIX AND I WILL GO WITH YOU...

SO WILL DOGMATIX! LOOK, HE'S ALREADY PICKED UP THE SCENT! HE'S MAKING STRAIGHT FOR THE RIVER!

SNIFF! SNIFF!

SURE ENOUGH...

HO, HO! NOT THE BEST TIME AND PLAICE FOR A ROMANTIC ROE, MY DEAR, BUT MULLET OVER, AND YOU'LL FIND, ONCE YOU'RE USED TO ME, I'M THE LIFE AND SOLE OF THE PARTY!

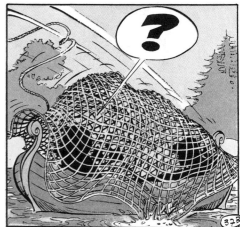

?

37^B

41

42

43

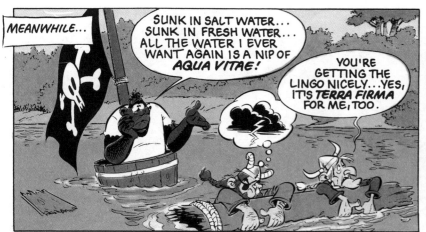

MEANWHILE...

SUNK IN SALT WATER... SUNK IN FRESH WATER... ALL THE WATER I EVER WANT AGAIN IS A NIP OF *AQUA VITAE!*

YOU'RE GETTING THE LINGO NICELY... YES, IT'S *TERRA FIRMA* FOR ME, TOO.

QUICK, LET'S GO AND SET MAJESTIX'S MIND AT REST!

IN TIMES OF TROUBLE SUCH AS THIS, IT IS ONLY RIGHT TO FORGET OUR DIFFERENCES, AND I FEEL FOR YOU, MAJESTIX!

THEY'RE BACK, WITH MELODRAMA!

OH, FATHER, HISTRIONIX ACTED LIKE A TRUE CHIEF!

I'M EXTREMELY GRATEFUL TO HISTRIONIX FOR HIS BRAVE ACTION, BUT THAT'S GOING A BIT TOO FAR, MY DEAR!

OH NO, IT ISN'T. AFTER ALL, HISTRIONIX IS THE SON OF A CHIEF!

SON OF A CHIEF MY FOOT!!! I'M THE ONLY REAL CHIEF AROUND HERE!

OH, FOR GOODNESS' SAKE, WE'VE HAD ENOUGH OF THIS! IF YOU MUST FIGHT FOR THE CHIEFTAINSHIP, KEEP IT BETWEEN THE TWO OF YOU!!!

MELODRAMA IS QUITE RIGHT! FIGHT IF YOU MUST, BUT LEAVE THE OTHER VILLAGERS OUT OF IT. THEY'VE HAD ENOUGH OF YOUR QUARRELS!

AND SOON AFTERWARDS...

NOW, YOU SENILE OLD DOTARD, I'LL SHOW YOU WHAT A REAL CHIEF CAN DO, AND WITH MY BARE HANDS!

YOU DYSPEPTIC OLD FOGY! YOU'RE IN FOR A SHOCK!

44

YOU'LL NEED A NEUTRAL UMPIRE. I VOLUNTEER TO REFEREE YOUR SINGLE COMBAT!

ACCORDING TO THE RULES, THE FIGHT MAY GO ON UNTIL SUNRISE TOMORROW. THE LOSER IS THE MAN WHO STAYS DOWN AFTER A COUNT OF 100! OFF YOU GO, AND MAY THE BEST MAN WIN THE PRIZE!

BONK!

CLONK!

V SESTERTII ON CLEVERDIX!

X ON MAJESTIX!

XV ON CLEVERDIX!

AS EVENING COMES ON, MANY OF THE AUDIENCE, TIRING OF THE SHOW, LEAVE THE RING.

THEY OUGHT TO REVISE THE RULES OF THESE PRIZEFIGHTS.

PAF! PAF!

IT'S LATE. I'M GOING TO BED, ASTERIX!

YAAAWN! SO ARE WE. DOGMATIX AND I DON'T TAKE MUCH INTEREST IN FIGHTS WHEN THERE AREN'T ANY ROMANS OR ANY BOARS.

ZZZZ!

EVEN ASTERIX IS UNABLE TO KEEP HIS EYES OPEN. ALL ALONE, IN THE MOONLIGHT, THE TWO CHIEFS ARE STILL EQUALLY MATCHED.

ZZZZZ!

PAF! PAF!

AND AT SUNRISE...

COCKADOODLE-DO!

?!?

RRRRR!

ZZZZ!

FRIENDS, FATE HAS DECIDED THE RESULT OF THE SINGLE COMBAT... NO ONE HAS WON AND NO ONE HAS LOST!

BUT YOU CAN HAVE A YOUNG, STRONG CHIEF IF YOU CHOOSE HISTRIONIX TO LEAD YOU, AND MELODRAMA WILL MAKE A WISE AND BEAUTIFUL CHIEF'S WIFE!

HURRAH! LONG LIVE HISTRIONIX! LONG LIVE MELODRAMA!

?.!.?

OH, WELL, I RATHER THINK ALL WE CAN DO IS GET DRESSED AGAIN!

YOU SAID IT, FAT-FACE!

REUNITED AT LAST, UNDER THE RULE OF THEIR NEW CHIEF HISTRIONIX, THE GAULS OF THE VILLAGE DIVERT PART OF THE NEARBY RIVER INTO THE DITCH, WHICH NO LONGER SERVES ANY USEFUL PURPOSE. AND NOW THERE IS NO PARTY OF THE RIGHT OR PARTY OF THE LEFT, ONLY A RIGHT BANK AND A LEFT BANK, RUNNING WATER ON EVERYONE'S DOORSTEP, AND FREEDOM FOR ALL THE VILLAGERS TO GO TO AND FRO.

THE BACK AND FORTH BRIDGE

THE CHILDREN CAN STILL GATHER THE FRUITS OF OTHER PEOPLE'S LABOURS WITH IMPUNITY...

SCRUNCH!

YOU'VE GOT NO RIGHT TO DO THAT! THAT'S MY TREE!!!

A NEW AND PRACTICAL USE IS FOUND FOR THE TWO GATEWAYS OF THE VILLAGE. HERE YOU SEE THE FIRST ONE-WAY SYSTEM KNOWN TO ANCIENT HISTORY!

AND SCHIZOPHRENIX'S HUT IS REBUILT AT LAST... THOUGH THE ARCHITECTS DID SLIP UP HERE AND THERE IN THEIR PLANS.

SPLOSH!

ANY IDEA WHAT BECAME OF THAT SCOUNDREL CODFIX?

NO, BUT I SHOULDN'T BE SURPRISED IF HE WAS STILL UP TO DIRTY WORK.

SURE ENOUGH, IN THE ROMAN CAMP...

WELL, SLAVE, HAVE YOU DONE THOSE VEGETABLES YET?

AND THE LAUNDRY? AND DON'T FORGET THE IRONING!

THE WEDDING OF MELODRAMA AND HISTRIONIX IS CELEBRATED AMIDST REJOICINGS FOR ALL AND BOARS FOR SOME.

SCRUNCH! SCRUNCH!

SCRUNCH! SCRUNCH!

THE TIME COMES TO SAY GOOD-BYE.

HOW CAN WE EVER THANK YOU FOR ALL WE OWE YOU?

YOU'RE HAPPY, AND THAT'S ALL THE THANKS WE NEED!

HUH!

47

The End

PRINTED IN BELGIUM BY
proost
INTERNATIONAL BOOK PRODUCTION